TWO ROMAN MICE

TWO ROMAN MICE

BY HORACE

· *Quintus Horatius Flaccus* ·

RETOLD AND ILLUSTRATED BY

Marilynne K. Roach

Thomas Y. Crowell Company | New York

Library of Congress Cataloging in Publication Data

Roach, Marilynne K.
    Two Roman mice.

    Based on a version of Aesop's fable about the country mouse and
the city mouse as it appeared in Horace's Satirae II, 6.
    Summary: When the town mouse and the city mouse exchange
visits, they discover they prefer very different ways of life.
    [1. Fables] I. Horatius Flaccus, Quintus. II. Title.
PZ8.2.F56Tw   [398.2]   74-32416
ISBN 0-690-00771-X

1   2   3   4   5   6   7   8   9   10

Parturient montes, nascetur rediculus mus. *Ars Poetica,* line 139

Once upon a time, in ancient Rome, there were two mice.

Rusticus lived in the hill country, a steep land shaggy with pines and holly. One day he invited his old friend Urbanus, who lived in the great city of Rome itself, to come and visit him.

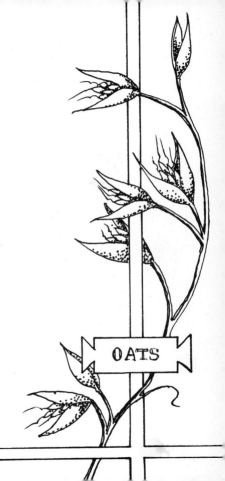

Life in the country was hard, but Rusticus wanted to be a generous host. He gathered a supper of chick-peas and oats, and brought cool water from a clear-flowing spring.

He even produced a special treat he had found under a farmer's table: one dried-up raisin and a scrap of bacon fat. Rusticus hoped that this would please Urbanus, who was trying not to make a face at the food.

SPELT

So Rusticus served the meal and the two mice settled themselves on clean straw, reclining to eat in the Roman manner. Rusticus ate his usual simple meal of spelt, vetch, and darnel grains. He left the best bits for his guest from the city.

DARNEL

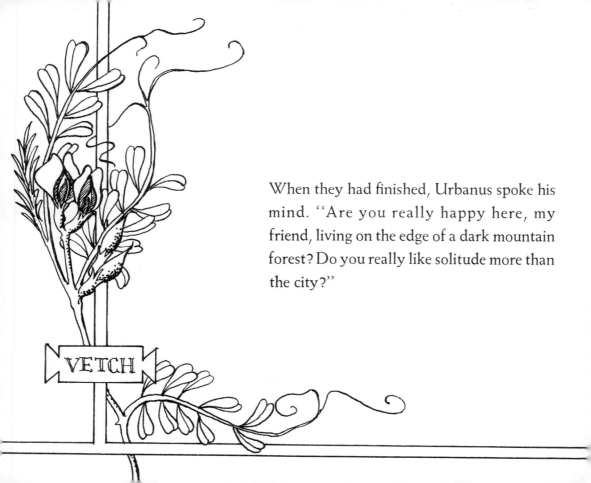

VETCH

When they had finished, Urbanus spoke his mind. "Are you really happy here, my friend, living on the edge of a dark mountain forest? Do you really like solitude more than the city?"

"Trust me. Life is short, so let us live as happily as we can. Come with me to Rome and enjoy the glories of city life."

Rusticus gave in. It sounded wonderful.
So the two mice set off for Rome together.

They entered the great city by night and
made their way to the mansion where
Urbanus lived.

In the elegant dining room lamplight gleamed on silver and fine glass, on scarlet drapery and dining couches inlaid with ivory. But best of all, there were baskets filled with leftovers stacked in the corner of the room.

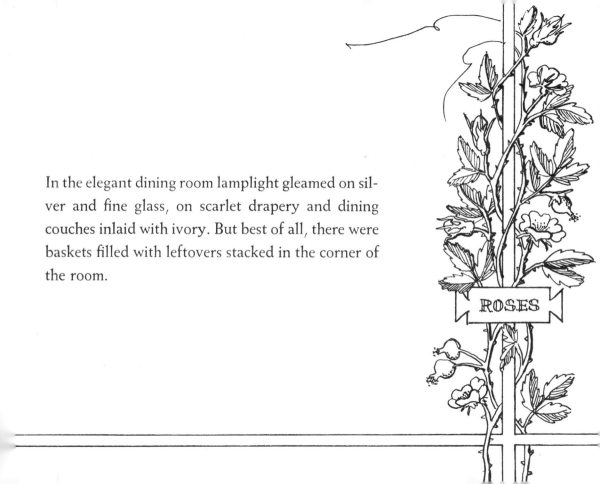

ROSES

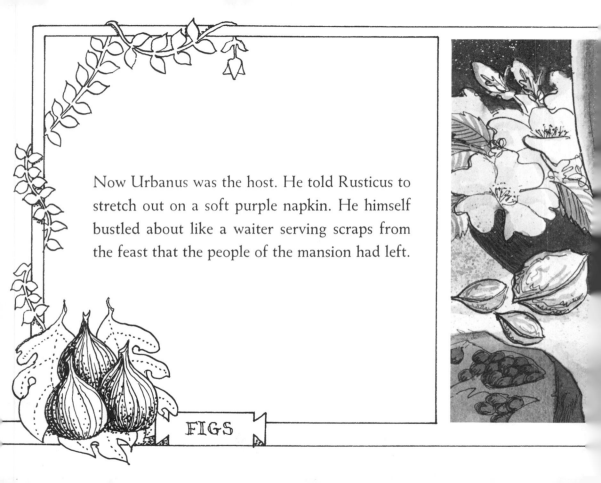

Now Urbanus was the host. He told Rusticus to stretch out on a soft purple napkin. He himself bustled about like a waiter serving scraps from the feast that the people of the mansion had left.

FIGS

They sampled lobster and asparagus tips, sipped honeyed wine, and nibbled at figs, dates, and the bright seeds of pomegranates.

POMEGRANATE

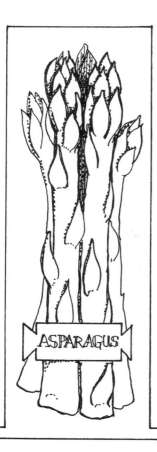

ASPARAGUS

Rusticus was delighted by it all.
He enjoyed being a happy guest for a change.

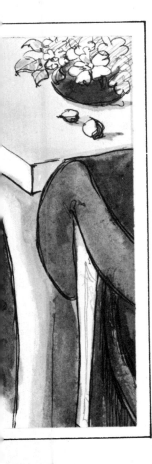

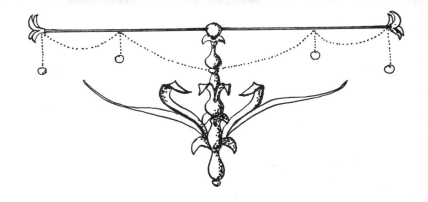

But suddenly a door opened with a crash and servants came in to clear off the tables. The mice jumped to the floor, but too late—the watchdogs had seen them!

In terror they ran from the room with the hounds chasing behind them, and the whole house was filled with loud, raucous barking. Breathless with fear the mice dodged through the garden and barely escaped up some vines to the top of a wall.

At last Rusticus gasped, "This city life isn't for me. Better seeds in the woods than feasts in a trap. You call this the good life? I don't, so farewell to Rome!"

And he ran back to his
simple country home in the hills.

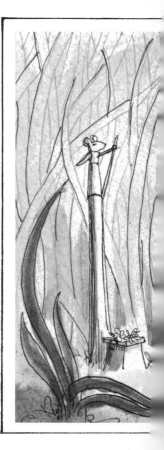

Quintus Horatius Flaccus, Satire II, vi

olim
rusticus urbanum murem mus paupere fertur
accepisse cavo, veterem vetus hospes amicum,
asper et attentus quaesitis, ut tamen artum
solveret hospitiis animum. quid multa? neque ille
sepositi ciceris nec longae indivit avenae,
aridum et ore ferens acinum semesaque lardi
frustra dedit, cupiens varia fastidia cena
vincere tangentis male singula dente superbo;
cum pater ipse domuś palea porrectus in horna
esset ador loliumque, dapis meliora relinquens.
tandem urbanus ad hunc, "quid te iuvat," inquit, "amice,
praerupti nemoris patientem vivere dorso?
vis tu homines urbemque feris praeponere silvis?
carpe viam, mihi crede, comes. terrestria quando
mortalis animas vivunt sortita, neque ulla est
aut magno aut parvo leti fuga, quo, bone, circa,
dum licet, in rebus iucundis vive beatus;
vive memor, quam sis aevi brevis." haec ubi dicta
agrestem pepulere, domo levis exsilit; inde
ambo propositum peragunt iter, urbis aventes
moenia nocturni subrepere.
Iamque tenebat
nox medium caeli spatium, cum ponit uterque
in locuplete domo vestigia, rubro ubi cocco
tincta super lectos canderet vestis eburnos,
multaque de magna superessent fercula cena,
quae procul exstructis inerant hesterna canistris.
ergo ubi purpurea porrectum in veste locavit
agrestem, veluti succinctus cursitat hospes
continuatque dapes, nec non verniliter ipsis
fungitur officiis, praelambens omne quod adfert
ille cubans gaudet mutata sorte bonisque
rebus agit laetum convivam, cum subito ingens
valvarum strepitus lectis excussit utrumque.
currere per totum pavidi conclave, magisque
exanimes trepidare, simul domus alta Molossis
personuit canibus. tum rusticus, "haud mihi vita
est opus hac," ait "et valeas: me silva cavusque
tutus ab insidiis tenui solabitur ervo."

NOTES

Quintus Horatius Flaccus, known in English as Horace, was born December 8, 65 B.C., at Venusia in southern Italy. His father, a former slave, moved the household to Rome so his promising son might receive the best possible education.

Later Horace was studying philosophy in Athens when civil war broke out after the assassination of Julius Caesar in 44 B.C. Many students, including Horace, joined Brutus' army, but on their defeat at Philippi in 42 B.C., Horace was obliged to throw away his shield and run for his life.

Returning to Rome, Horace found himself alone in the world and the family farm in Venusia confiscated. He managed to become a scribe in the quaestor's office, a sort of clerk-accountant, and because of the job's dullness and his own poverty he began writing poetry in his spare time.

After four years his poems came to the attention of the rising poet Virgil, who, in turn, showed them to his patron, Maecenas. This man not only sponsored some of the best literary talents of his day, but served as chief adviser to Octavius Caesar, who later became the emperor Augustus. A meeting was arranged at which Maecenas said little and Horace stammered much. After a nine-month silence, Maecenas became Horace's patron.

During his career Horace published collections of *Odes*, *Epodes*, *Satires*, and *Epistles*. He was the first to write successful Latin poetry in Classical Greek forms.

About 33 B.C. Maecenas gave Horace a country retreat, a small estate in the Sabine Hills, which became the poet's beloved "Sabine farm." *Satire* II, vi, a poem of thanks, contrasts the peace of the farm with the bustle of Rome, and ends with the fable of the city mouse and the country mouse.

Horace died on November 27, 8 B.C., and was buried in Rome on the Esquiline Hill near his friend Maecenas. The exact site is unknown, but, as Horace himself wrote, his poetry is "a monument more lasting than bronze."

Two ROMAN MICE is a fairly literal translation of Horace's *Satire* II, vi, somewhat adapted for non-Romans. The city supper menu, for example, was added to balance the country meal's list of seeds and scraps. The illustrations also continue the translation. For instance, the flat basket of scraps is a *canistrum* like the ones in the "Triumph of Dionysus" mosaic in the Sousse Museum in North Africa; the folding doors which slam open are similar to the *valvae* in the House of the Bicentenary in Herculaneum; the watchdogs are Molossian hounds, a now-extinct, mastiff-like breed. Rusticus gets water from Horace's beloved Bandusian Spring, and the Sabine Hills behind the mice as they leave are viewed from Horace's villa, the site of which has been excavated. The decorative borders are patterned after wall frescoes typical of the period, like those found in Pompeii and Herculaneum.

ABOUT MARILYNNE K. ROACH

Marilynne Roach bought her drafting board with the money she received for a set of cartoons on classical themes that were published in the magazine *Auxilium Latinum*. That was in her first year in college, but her interest in art—and in classical subjects—began when she was in grade school.

Ms. Roach was born in Cambridge, Massachusetts, and grew up in nearby Watertown, attending its schools and haunting its library system. In 1968 she was graduated from the Massachusetts College of Art with a Bachelor of Fine Arts degree. She has worked as a designer of mosaic murals and is now a full-time free-lance artist and writer. Two ROMAN MICE is the first book that Marilynne Roach has both written and illustrated; an earlier tale, *The Mouse and the Song*, with illustrations by Joseph Low, was published in 1974.